Bartholomew's Blessing

To Christian
—S.S.T.

To Kelly
—M.M.

Bartholomew's Blessing
Text copyright © 2004 by Stephanie S. Tolan
Illustrations copyright © 2004 by Margie Moore
Manufactured in China. All rights reserved.
www.harperchildrens.com

Library of Congress Cataloging-in-Publication Data
Tolan, Stephanie S.
Bartholomew's Blessing / by Stephanie S. Tolan ; illustrated by Margie Moore.
p.   cm.
Summary: In this Christmas story, a mouse is invited by an angel and a fox to make the journey to
Bethlehem and be blessed by the Christ Child.
ISBN 0-06-001197-1 — ISBN 0-06-001198-X (lib. bdg.)
I. Jesus Christ—Nativity—Juvenile fiction. [1. Jesus Christ—Nativity—Fiction. 2. Christmas—Fiction.
3. Mice—Fiction. 4. Animals—Fiction.]
I. Moore, Margie, ill. II. Title.
PZ7.T5735 Bar 2003   2001051737
[E]—dc21   CIP
AC

Typography by Stephanie Bart-Horvath
1 2 3 4 5 6 7 8 9 10
❖
First Edition

Bartholomew's Blessing

by Stephanie S. Tolan

illustrated by Margie Moore

HarperCollinsPublishers

Bartholomew Mouse woke up shivering and snuggled deeper into his nest of dried grass. The night was very cold— very cold and very noisy.

He opened one eye. What was that light?

*B*linking and yawning, he crept to his front door and peered out. A donkey trotted by, nearly squashing Bartholomew flat.

"What's happening?" Bartholomew called after it. "Where are you going?"

The donkey didn't answer.

Bartholomew sighed. He was a small animal, used to being ignored.

*T*wo sheep hurried past. "Please," Bartholomew called to them. "What's happening? Where is everybody going?"

The sheep were humming along with the music that floated down out of the sky. They did not hear his voice.

Bartholomew heard the sound of wings and ducked back into his hole. It was almost as bright as day, bright enough for hawks to be about.

But this was not a hawk. "Glad tidings!" the angel said as she hovered near his door.

Bartholomew blinked. "I beg your pardon?"

"Good news! The Prince of Peace is born this night. He is going to bless the animals. Come!"

"Come where?" Bartholomew asked.

"To the stable," she said, and was gone in a flurry of feathers.

Bartholomew stood for a moment, chewing the tip of his paw. Surely no prince would bless a creature as small and unimportant as himself.

A fox bounded over his head. "Come along," he said, "or you'll miss the blessing." The fox had not pounced on him, had not gobbled him up. A strange night it was—and wonderful. An angel and a fox had invited him to come along.

"A newborn prince," he muttered to himself. "I must take a gift." He hurried back to his nest and got the barley head he had intended for his breakfast.

It was no trouble finding the way to the stable. A star he had never seen before shone like a brilliant fire in the sky. Bartholomew had only to follow the other animals hurrying past him.

He stopped beneath a sweet gum tree. The star's light shone on a frost-covered seed pod. "Beautiful!" Bartholomew breathed. "The Prince will love it!" He put the barley head between his teeth, picked up the seed pod, and hurried onward.

As he went, the night grew colder. It began to snow, the flakes sparkling in the light of the star.

Ahead of him something on the ground sparkled even more brightly than the snowflakes. It was a stone, gold and red and glittering. "This is more beautiful yet," Bartholomew said. "The Prince must have it, too."

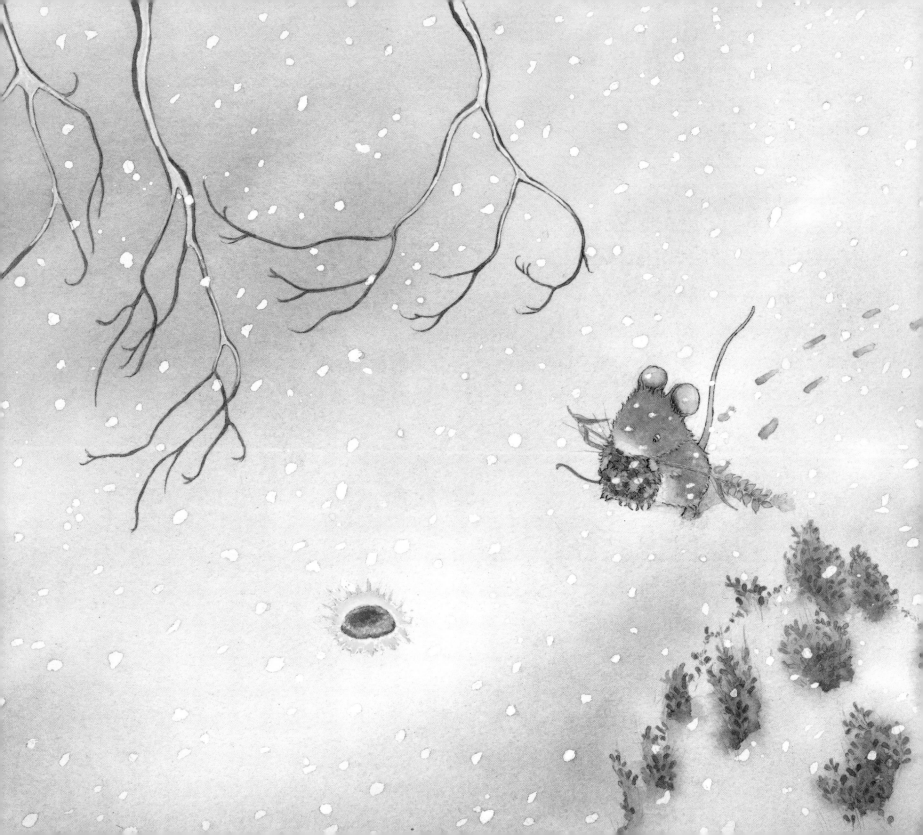

*B*artholomew struggled on in the deepening snow. Now he could see the stable ahead, bright with starlight. Animals were moving toward it from all directions. Some of the sheep had brought their shepherds, he noticed. Perhaps the Prince would bless the humans, too. Angels soared overhead, filling the air with song.

All that was left between Bartholomew and the stable was a stream, its water gurgling and splashing between stones and thin crusts of ice. Bartholomew stood for a moment on the bank, looking for a way to cross. Then he saw a perfect icicle hanging from a branch over the stream. It gleamed silver. The most beautiful gift of all, Bartholomew thought. Balancing stone and pod in one paw, he reached . . .

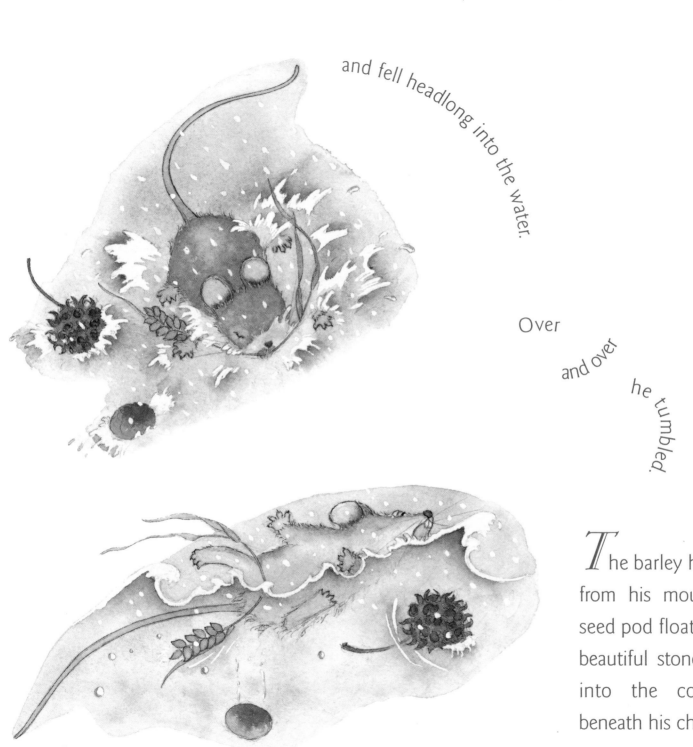

and fell headlong into the water.

Over
and over
he tumbled.

*T*he barley head was torn from his mouth, and the seed pod floated away. The beautiful stone disappeared into the cold darkness beneath his churning paws.

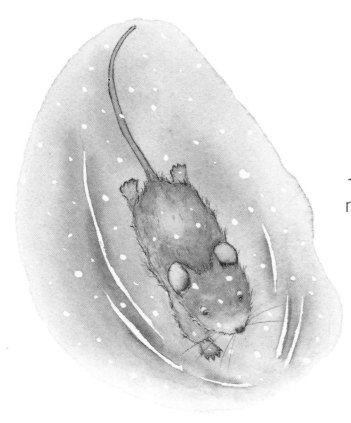

At last Bartholomew, swimming mightily, reached the other bank.

He dragged himself out of the water and sat dejectedly in the snow. He had nothing at all to take the Prince. He shivered as he pushed himself to his feet.

"The Prince will not notice me," Bartholomew told himself, "but I've come this far. I can't go home without seeing him."

*I*nside, the stable was filled with the soft sounds of the animals breathing. Bartholomew, wet, bedraggled, and shivering, made his way forward between the legs of the other creatures.

In a manger full of golden straw a baby lay, waving his hands in the light that surrounded him. Bartholomew caught his breath in wonder. This was a baby—a prince—worthy of all the gifts he had meant to bring.

A drop of cold water ran down Bartholomew's nose. He sneezed.
The baby turned his head and looked at Bartholomew with bright,
dark eyes. The baby smiled.

Warmth and light filled Bartholomew. He felt his fur dry and fluff. He felt himself grow larger. Soon he was as big as a sheep—a donkey—a camel.

Bartholomew, the biggest creature in the stable, smiled back.

*A*nd the night was filled with blessings.